D0659677

Endorsements for Jazzy's Quest

"Finally, an early chapter book that validates what many adopted kids experience – issues with identity-building, challenges in fitting in, and the question of special-vs.-different. I suspect many readers will feel a connection with heroine Jazzy, loved and supported by both her birth and adoptive families, but still facing a struggle. The kids will think they're just reading an engaging story, but the parents will know there's so much more going on than just good kid-lit."

– Lori Holden
author of *The Open-Hearted Way to Open Adoption: Helping Your Child Grow Up Whole*

"Jazzy felt different in a yucky way until she discovered her differences from her adoptive family were in reality gifts in disguise that she could give to others. To top it off, she experiences the joy of having a fellow adoptee friend. Your adopted kids will love this!"

– Sherrie Eldridge
Author of *Twenty Things Adopted Kids Wish Their Adoptive Parents Knew*

"*Jazzy's Quest* is heartfelt, engaging and absolutely lovely. Goldman and Bond not only wrote a story to entertain, but one that is necessary in a world where being 'different' is so often looked at as a negative thing. Well done and definitely worth a read!"

– Jenna Busch, Founder of Legion of Leia

"Jazzy, a spunky fourth-grader, yearns to fit in. As an adoptee, she feels like the sour note in her musically talented family. Her efforts to perform with them prove disastrous. Young readers will recognize a piece of their own struggle for acceptance and belonging. They'll root for Jazzy to power through her fear and doubts to discover her hidden talents. Enthusiasm, strength and confidence reveal exactly where Jazzy belongs."

– Gayle H. Swift
co-founder of GIFT Family Services,
author of *ABC, Adoption & Me*

"Jazzy is the type of character that will leap off the page and right into your children's lives. If only she could come over for an actual play-date! And, as the white, adoptive father of two African-American kids, I'm so grateful to the authors for bringing to life a character and story as rooted in diverse portrayals of family, people, and ability as Jazzy's Quest is. This is a great kids book – for families and kids of all kinds."

– Seth Matlins
Father of two transracial adoptees

"The school talent show is just a few weeks away, and Jazzy Armstrong is nervous. What will her talent be? But more to the point, where do interests and talents actually come from — your adoptive family, your birth family, or somewhere deep inside yourself? Jazzy's quest to understand who she is leads her on a journey of self-discovery; the ultimate conclusion reached is that fitting in can mean being different.

This warm and insightful early chapter book addresses some of the unique identity issues faced by adopted children in a way that will nonetheless resonate with all children, because all children experience the growing pains of defining who they are relative to their parents and siblings. Adopted children will find special affirmation and joy in the story of Jazzy's talent show performance because she shows readers that being adopted does not solely define her, but that it does enrich her in ways that knit together as she triumphantly takes the stage and shows everyone what it means to dig deep and come out smiling!"

– Lori Day
author of *Her Next Chapter: How Mother-Daughter Book Clubs Can Help Girls Navigate Malicious Media, Risky Relationships, Girl Gossip, and So Much More*

Jazzy's Quest: Adopted and Amazing
by Carrie Goldman & Juliet C. Bond, LCSW
Illustrated by Gabrielle Terbush

Printed in the United States of America.
Published by Marcinson Press, Jacksonville, Florida
© Copyright 2015 by Carrie Goldman & Juliet Bond, LCSW

ISBN 978-0-9893732-8-9

Published by
Marcinson Press
10950-60 San Jose Blvd., Suite 136
Jacksonville, FL 32223 USA
http://www.marcinsonpress.com

Jazzy's

QUEST

ADOPTED
AND
AMAZING!

To our **AMAZING** kids
Jacob, Lilly, Katie, Casey,
Annie Rose and Cleo

and to some of the
AMAZING loves of our lives
Kevin, Andrew, Mairita,
Toms, and Tomass.

Introduction

by Travis Langley, Ph.D., Author of "Star Wars Psychology" and "Batman & Psychology"

With something as simple as a song, the authors immediately pull us into Jasmine's seat in the car and her place in the world. We quickly get to know Jazzy and we feel for her. She is an interesting and sympathetic soul. Each initial discovery raises many questions in the readers' minds.

Music bonds her adoptive family together as The Amazing Armstrongs and makes her feel left out, and so it is not without irony that her nickname evokes jazz. Even the dog's name, Sing, becomes a compromise between her family's musical interest and Jasmine's love of Star Wars characters. The dog, Sing, howls when Jasmine tries to sing.

Jazzy's quest to find her talent is a quest to find her place in her family, to be amazing along with them. This caring child feels concern that others, like her wheelchair-bound friend Alec, might feel left out or truly get left out by others. People can feel alien in many different ways, for many different reasons. People can connect, however, when they realize that feeling alien is something they have in common.

Feeling alien makes the characters in the fiction Jasmine loves appeal to her all the more. Aliens fill Star Wars, so much so that "alien" is normal. Princess Leia, also adopted in her infancy by a loving family, provides Jasmine with a role model: a fellow adoptee and a girl who grows up to become a strong leader and maybe even a Jedi.

Fiction is a powerful thing – on several levels, in this case. Fiction from the real world inspires this delightful girl in her fictional world, and her story can, in turn, inspire many people in our world.

This is a wonderful, captivating story. When it ended, I did not want to stop reading. The writing style is vivid. The story offers insight into childhood, adoption, and family life. Readers can learn a few things about adoption itself, including open adoption. This is an important work for all readers: children and adults, families of many kinds, oh so many people who feel like square pegs in round holes, and also the round pegs who can benefit from a glimpse into lives whose shapes have corners.

TABLE OF CONTENTS

Dear Reader,

As an adoptive mom and a children's book writer, we knew that there weren't many early chapter books about adopted kids. But imagine how surprised we were to find out that there was only one!

That's when we decided to write the *Jazzy's Quest* series. Jazzy is a fourth-grade girl who loves her family, but she still thinks it is hard to be adopted. Jazzy feels different from her parents and sisters, and she wants to find out what makes her special.

To help us create the character of Jazzy, we talked a lot to Carrie's daughter, Katie, who is also adopted. Katie helped us understand how sometimes it can be painful to be the only adopted child in her family.

We also wanted to include diverse characters in our book, so Jazzy's birth family is Latino, and her best friend, Alec, is a boy who uses a wheelchair. There are all different kinds of amazing people in this world, and children's books should reflect that!

All our best,
Carrie Goldman and Juliet Bond

Chapter One
Jasmine's soundtrack

Jazzy dug her feet into her sister's seat as her mother drove to school. It was supposed to be Jazzy's turn to ride in that seat. Sometimes, Jazzy wondered how she fit into her family.

"You are my suuunshiiine!"

Her mom and sister belted out their favorite song.

"Sing with us, Jazzy!" Mom shouted over the music.

"I am," Jasmine said. She stared out the window, not singing.

The day was sunny, but inside, Jasmine felt more like clouds and blue-grey skies. Mom and Sophie sang together, their voices wound around each other in ribbons of perfect harmony. Jasmine wiggled her toes deeper into the seat.

"Hey, watch your feet," Sophie said. Her copper ponytail bounced as she swung around to face Jasmine. Both of her sisters had red hair.

"Sorry," Jasmine mumbled, twisting her finger through one of her own black curls.

Sophie reached back to nudge Jasmine's leg. "You're not singing."

"I am singing. You just can't hear me." Jasmine whispered the words to the song, scowling at the way her voice sounded. She sort of hated to sing. She could not sing like her sisters or her parents. It was more like a howling cat or air being squeezed from a tire.

But her family was crazy about music. They even had a small band. They were The Amazing Armstrongs. Jasmine didn't want to be in the band. She wished she knew what made her amazing.

"C'mon, Jazzy," Mom pleaded.

"You make me haaaapy, when skies are grey," Jasmine mouthed the words without making a sound.

As the girls tumbled out of the car, Mom half-sang and half-shouted, "Have a great day!"

Jasmine started off towards the blue school doors. "Oh, wait!" Mom called. She leaned out of the car window. "I talked to Antonia last night. She and Carlos can make it to The Walnut Room next week."

Antonia and Carlos were Jasmine's birth mother and brother. Every year, they met at The Walnut Room in Chicago for a special holiday dinner.

Jasmine smiled and clutched her Star Wars backpack to her chest. "Okay, that's great," she said. "Bye Mom. Love you."

Swinging her backpack, she walked into school. Jasmine loved seeing her birth family. But thinking about them could make her stomach twist a little. Jasmine didn't know any other adopted kids. Sometimes it made her feel special, but other times she felt alone.

Outside Ms. Weir's classroom, Jasmine hung her coat on a hook. Kids swarmed around her, and the hallway smelled like hot oatmeal.

"Hey, Jasmine," called her friend Alec

Waldon as he swiveled through a cluster of kids. "Check this out." Alec's cheeks were so flushed with excitement that his freckles had almost disappeared. He reached into a pocket of his wheelchair to pull out a yellow flyer. "There's a community talent show coming up in three weeks. Are you signing up?"

Jasmine ignored the paper, turning her attention instead to something metal that jangled as it fell out of Alec's backpack.

"What's this?" Jasmine asked. Two shiny rings banged against one another as she picked them up.

"Oh," Alec waved a hand. "I got that for my birthday. It's some magic trick from my grandma. I guess you're supposed to separate the rings. But look at this." He thrust out the yellow paper again.

Still focused on the rings, Jasmine held the bigger ring steady and rotated the smaller one. She pushed the ends together, and the rings clinked softly as they fell apart.

"How did you do that?" Alec asked with wide eyes.

She shrugged and handed the trick back to Alec.

"Keep it," he laughed, shaking his head. "It's been driving me crazy!"

Jasmine dropped the rings into her bag. She could probably use them to make a cool belt for her new Princess Leia costume. "Thanks."

"So, are you going to do the talent show?"

Jasmine knew about the talent show. It was all her sisters had been talking about for a week. She shrugged. "What are you going to do for the talent show?"

Alec grinned. "I'm an incredible wheelchair break-dancer!" He hopped his wheelchair back and forth in tiny, jerky movements. "I've been taking lessons for years."

Jasmine laughed. "You are pretty good at that!"

Two lockers away, Haley Smith rolled her eyes and whispered to Greta Williams. Jasmine watched Alec as he glanced at the girls and turned back to her. Sometimes, kids pestered Alec because of his wheelchair.

"Thanks," he said. "So, what will you do?"

Jasmine walked alongside Alec as he wheeled forward. "Will you sing with your family?" he asked. "I love The Amazing Armstrongs!"

The two friends entered their classroom. "Remember last year when your parents and sisters did that number with seven different instruments?"

"Yeah," Jasmine said. "They are pretty amazing…" her voice trailed off.

Alec patted Jasmine's sleeve. "You'll think of something," he said.

"Right," she answered.

Chapter Two
Trouble With Music

After school, Jasmine dropped her backpack in the entryway. She could hear the cheerful sounds of guitar and piano from the den. She poked her head into the room.

"We're practicing for the talent show!" her sister May shouted. "Do you want to join The Amazing Armstrongs?"

"I'll think about it." Jasmine bent down to pet her dog. "Right now I am so hungry, I could eat one of Sing's dog biscuits." Sing's name had been a compromise when Jasmine and her sisters got the dog two years ago. Jasmine wanted to name the dog after one of her favorite

Star Wars characters while her sisters wanted something musical.

"What about Aurra Sing?" Jasmine had suggested. Aurra Sing was a fierce bounty hunter in the Star Wars series. She had an awesome collection of lightsabers that she took from every Jedi that she'd battled. Jasmine admired her ability to carry out the most dangerous tasks, even though she chose to work for bad guys.

"Cool name!" May and Sophie had said in unison. "Let's call her Sing for short."

Sing yelped and Jasmine smiled. Unlike the Star Wars character Aurra Sing, Sing the dog was sweet natured and wouldn't kill a flea, much less a Jedi. Jasmine went into the kitchen to assemble a plate of cheese and crackers. Sing whined at Jasmine's feet, begging for bits of cheese.

In the kitchen, Mom was searching for an afternoon snack too. "How was your day, sweetie?"

She gave Jasmine a quick squeeze as she pulled a jar of pickles from the fridge.

"Can I take guitar lessons?" Jasmine asked.

"Of course you can." Mom struggled to open the pickle jar. She handed the jar to Jasmine, who hit the side of it with her hand. The tin top made a popping sound as it released some air. Then Jasmine spun the top off with ease.

"Thanks!" Mom said. "Um," she paused. "Jazzy, do you think you would like guitar? You hated the flute."

"I don't know," Jasmine said. "I need to figure out what to do for the talent show."

"You could just sing with us." Mom crunched on a pickle.

"Maybe…"

"Well, guitar is a good idea," Mom said. "It was the first instrument I learned to play and I loved it. You can borrow mine until we know for sure whether or not you like it."

On Friday, Jasmine had her first guitar lesson. The strings of the guitar made angry, twanging noises when she tried to play Mary Had a Little Lamb. The teacher said, "You'll need to rehearse finger placement and chords at home. Don't worry, no one is a great guitar player at first."

For a full week, Jasmine practiced guitar until her fingers grew small blisters. Setting the guitar down, Jasmine glared at it. It's going to be impossible to learn this in three weeks, she worried. Jasmine dragged the guitar pick across her music book.

After dinner, Jasmine snuggled next to her dad on the couch as they settled in to watch the newest episode of Star Wars Rebels. A giant bowl of popcorn filled the room with the comforting smell of melted butter.

"Dad?" Jasmine asked.

He plunged his hand into the popcorn bowl. "Yeah?"

"Was it easy for you to learn to play guitar?"

Dad paused the show. "I wouldn't say it was easy, no. Still, I loved it so much that I wanted to play it every day. It was the first thing I did when I got home from school and the only thing I wanted to do on the weekends. I never played baseball or loved football like my brothers. For me, it was always music."

"Oh," Jasmine sighed. "I don't feel that way

about guitar."

Jasmine's dad wrapped his long arm across her shoulders. "Your thing doesn't have to be guitar, kiddo."

Jasmine looked at the Star Wars characters frozen in action on her TV screen. She picked up the remote control and pushed play. She'd think about the talent show tomorrow.

Chapter Three
Sign Up Day

Saturday morning, Sophie and May sat in the living room practicing their duet for the talent show. "Maybe I'll join your act," Jasmine said.

"Great," Sophie said, handing Jasmine a sheet of music. Jasmine hesitated a minute and then joined in. Her voice sounded very loud. Sophie and May looked at each other. Sing began to howl. She sounded as if she were crooning along. Jasmine suspected that her dog was a better singer than Jasmine was.

"Jazzy, that's a good start. Maybe try it a little softer," May suggested.

"Okay," Jasmine said.

For three days, Jasmine joined her sisters for their rehearsals. Every time Jasmine sang, Sing howled in time. On the fourth day, Jasmine balled up her fists, crumpling the music. "I sound awful!"

May and Sophie exchanged looks. "It's not that bad," May said.

"It is that bad," Jasmine said. "I'm ruining your song. The dog is more in tune than I am."

Despite herself, Sophie giggled.

"I only have two and a half weeks before the talent show!" Jasmine slammed the door as she left the parlor.

In her room, she pulled out the Princess Leia costume she'd been working on for months, the one Leia wore in Cloud City. That was one of Jazzy's favorite scenes from The Empire Strikes Back. She'd finished the red silk top and matching pants, but the cape was so intricate that she'd spent weeks trying to get the embroidery just right. Sewing the elaborate costume calmed her down. She held the cape up, admiring the carefully threaded gold patterns against the silvery fabric. This year, she'd worn the classic white Leia costume for Halloween. Next year, she would wear this. She could hardly wait.

Leia, like Jasmine, had been adopted as a baby. She grew up to be a strong leader and one of the few female Jedi knights. Jasmine picked up one of her Leia lightsabers and began to practice fighting off the evil Sith Lord.

At the talent show sign-up, she saw Alec filling out his forms. "Hey Jasmine!" he smiled. "Have you figured out what you're going to do for the show?"

"Um," she hesitated. In the corner of the room, an old tuba leaned against the wall. "It's a surprise," she muttered.

Haley and Greta entered the room laughing. "Oh, Alec." Haley approached Alec's wheelchair. "Did you sign up for something?"

"Yes," Alec handed his music to Greta, who was the stage manager of the community talent show.

Greta read Alec's entry on the whiteboard, "Dancing?" she asked.

"Hmmm…" Haley ran her fingers across one

of the Star Wars stickers Jazzy had placed on Alec's wheelchair. "I didn't know that people like you could dance."

Alec said nothing. Backing his wheelchair towards the exit, Alec turned away from Haley and Greta.

"Show us some of those cool wheelchair breakdance moves," Greta giggled.

Suddenly, the old theater felt very warm. Jasmine's face was sweaty. She wanted to leave, but she still hadn't signed up for anything.

Alec fumbled with the doorknob. "I got it," Jazzy said. She pushed opened the heavy, wood door to let Alec pass through.

After Alec left, Jazzy walked slowly back to the whiteboard. Haley's mother, who was in charge of the community talent show, entered the room.

"Haley, I need you up here." Ms. Smith pulled a microphone onto the stage. "Let's see if this old microphone works. The announcer has to be prepared."

On the board, Jazzy stared at the categories of talent. She ignored the column for dance.

Jasmine's dancing was more like tripping and falling over.

"Testing!" Haley shouted from the stage.

There was a section for people who did magic, one for musicians, another for actors and one that was just called "other."

"Testing, one two three!" Haley howled into the microphone.

None of the categories were right for Jazzy. On the sign-up board, she wrote "Jasmine Armstrong: TUBA."

Chapter Four
Totally Tuba

At home, Jasmine found her dad in the den.

"Hey, Dad. Don't we have a tuba somewhere?"

Dad looked up from a stack of papers. His glasses hung from the end of his nose like a pair of sleds inching down a steep hill. "That old thing? It's in the garage, but it's been stuck in its case for years."

"Thanks, Dad. I'll see if I can get it open."

Her dad chuckled. "If anyone can, it's you, Jazzy. Remember how you figured out how to remove the pipe and fix the sink after May dumped all of that pasta down the disposal?"

Jasmine remembered the rubbery noodles, clogged in a gluey mess inside the pipe. Dad had taken a picture and posted it over the sink to remind everyone not to put pasta in the disposal.

"Or how you programmed the TV to record all of our favorite shows at just the right times?"

That was an easy one. Jazzy used the guide that came with the TV to figure out which commands would tape the right shows in the order her family preferred.

"That saved a lot of arguments among you girls." Dad pushed his glasses up with one finger. "Then there was the time your Ewok action figure got sucked into the vacuum cleaner, and you took the whole hose apart to..."

Her dad was still reminiscing as Jasmine walked away. She could get the tuba out of its case.

Jasmine found the old tuba case propped up in the corner of the garage. Examining the jammed lock, Jasmine saw the problem.

She used a screwdriver to loosen a few of the tumblers inside the rusted lock and pried it open. The lock squealed as it popped apart. Lifting the heavy case, Jasmine struggled to get the giant instrument out. Sing cocked her head as Jasmine reached around to finger the valves. Placing her lips against the mouthpiece, Jasmine blew as hard as she could. An angry belching noise exploded from the bell of the tuba.

Jasmine pushed the tuba off of her lap. "Ugh!" she moaned to a quizzical Sing. "This is never going to work. I didn't get the musical talent that comes from my family."

She buried her face in the dog's thick fur. "Maybe I just don't belong!" Sing licked the salty tears that dripped off Jasmine's nose.

"What's wrong?" May asked. She stood in the doorway with her head cocked to one side.

"I can't play an instrument," Jasmine said. "I can't sing."

The dog's ears pricked up at the sound of her name. "I'll never be an Amazing Armstrong."

Frowning, May sat on a nearby box. "You know, Jasmine… I'm a terrible chess player. My friends all think it's weird that I hate mayonnaise. And I get really shy around teachers."

"Mom does say you never raise your hand in class."

"Never," May admitted.

"But those are all things that make you different from people outside of our family. I'm different from everyone inside of our family. I'm different from all of you. I'm the only adopted kid in our family."

May tugged at her green t-shirt. "It's true, you are the only adopted kid. But, even in our family, we aren't all the same. You and Dad are the only people in our family who love Star Wars."

Sophie chimed in as she entered the garage, "And you and Mom are the only ones who like pickles."

"I hate pickles," May shuddered.

Sophie sunk down on the bench next to Jasmine. Sophie smelled like soap and her hair was wet from a recent shower. "You and I always win at Dominoes."

Jazzy nodded.

"Dad always says he's going to win and then we beat him," she said.

The sun outside the open garage door was turning orange, throwing a soft glow around the sisters. Jasmine rested her head against Sophie's shoulder. "Yeah," she said softly. "But I'm still not an Amazing Armstrong."

Chapter Five

Dinner at the Walnut Room

That night, Jasmine pulled on a sparkly sweater for the Walnut Room supper with her birth and adoptive families. The Armstrongs arrived a few minutes early and got in line to be seated. The wide dining room was filled with dark walnut posts, matching tables, and a long bar. The waiters raced back and forth in white shirts, carrying trays of steaming pies and carefully balanced cups of hot cocoa with towers of whipped cream. As they stood in line waiting for a table, Antonia and Carlos dashed towards Jasmine with big grins.

They had also dressed up for this dinner.

Antonia wore a silky blue dress with a silvery necklace and Carlos sported a red bow tie to go with his button-down shirt. Sophie and Dad gave high fives to little Carlos.

"Hello!" Antonia lifted Jasmine into a bear hug. "Jazzy, you have grown at least three inches since summer!"

"I've grown taller too!" Carlos said. "And look! I put gel in my hair." His slick curls gleamed in the blue light of the Walnut Room.

"Looking good," Jasmine said. She eyed Antonia's hair, the exact same shade as Carlos' and Jasmine's. Maybe there was a special talent Jasmine inherited from her birth family.

The host approached Jasmine, Carlos and Antonia. "Table for three?" he asked, commenting to Antonia, "Your daughter looks just like you."

"Oh, thanks," Antonia said and looked at Jasmine's mom. "Actually," Antonia began.

Jasmine's mom winked, her eyes twinkling with pride, "We are both her mother," they said together.

The waiter's cheeks got red. "Oh, um, sure.

Well, right this way."

Jasmine loved having two mothers who were crazy about her. But she knew that, to some people, it seemed strange. She wanted to be amazing without seeming too different. Some people asked questions about why Jasmine didn't look exactly like her family.

When they learned she was adopted, most people assumed she didn't know anything about Carlos and Antonia. But in reality, her birth family was an important part of her life, because hers was an open adoption. Most people were surprised to learn that she visited her birth family.

Jasmine looked at Carlos, then May and Sophie. Were they ever sad that they only had one mom? Did having two moms make Jazzy amazing?

At dinner, she turned to Carlos. "Do you play any instruments?" she asked.

"Nope." He blew on a mouthful of his chicken potpie. "I like sports. Do you play any sports?"

"Not really," Jasmine answered. "I played

one season of soccer, but I never liked all the kicking and getting kicked and stuff. Does Antonia play an instrument?"

"I don't think so," Carlos said. "Sometimes she sings in the shower…"

Antonia leaned over and said, "I took piano lessons as a kid, and I was actually pretty good, but I never liked to practice."

"Me neither," Jasmine whispered. She didn't want her parents to overhear. At the table behind theirs, a baby wailed. "I'm not sure what my talent is," Jasmine said, staring at her mashed potatoes.

Antonia smiled at the crying baby. "Your great birth grandmother, Abuela Ana, made amazing tortillas. She used to invite her neighbors over for big dinners where everyone brought different fillings and she made the tacos. Her meals were better than anything you could order in a restaurant," she said.

Jasmine didn't have any interest in cooking. She'd made brownies once and the recipe was so complicated that she couldn't keep the ingredients and amounts straight. They came out burnt on the edges and raw in the middle. She pushed her turkey around her plate. "So," Jasmine blurted, "what else are you good at?"

Antonia smiled. "I love arranging flowers for celebrations like weddings and Mother's Day, which is why I started my business. But I think you can be good at anything you like. You just have to work at it."

"What if you don't like it?" Jasmine asked.

By now, Mom had overheard Jasmine's conversation with Antonia. She leaned across the table. "If it isn't something you have to do, then it's okay to look for something else."

Mom winked at Jazzy.

"But what if nobody likes the same thing you do?" Jasmine asked.

Antonia looked at Jasmine and paused before she said, "It's okay to be different. What's important is to follow your own path and become excellent at whatever you like."

May piped in, "Jasmine has been trying to find an instrument she likes."

"Like the Amazing Armstrongs!" Carlos gushed. He'd been to one of their concerts and couldn't stop talking about it afterwards.

"I don't really like playing instruments," Jasmine said.

May stabbed a piece of meatloaf. "I wish I could be more like you, Jasmine! You can take apart anything and fix it. You can find a random piece of metal and turn it into a realistic Star Wars toy."

Jasmine's stomach unclenched a little. She was pretty good at fixing things. Plus, she'd made most of her Star Wars costumes and accessories by herself. Her mom and sisters couldn't sew, and her dad was hopeless at constructing things.

"Hey, it's the holiday fairy!" Sophie interrupted as a young woman in a blue tulle gown approached their table. The fairy sprinkled glitter over each person's head.

"A little magic for each of you!" the fairy cried. "Make a wish."

Jasmine closed her eyes and wished. Mom asked the fairy to take a photo of everyone. "Say fairy dust!" shouted the fairy as she snapped the picture.

"Fairy dust!" they said, laughing.

Jasmine watched the fairy as she moved onto the next table. The fairy tossed a handful of sparkles above a little girl's head. A few glittering pieces stuck to the child's hair, and Jasmine remembered that she wanted to add something shiny to her half-finished Queen Padme headpiece.

Suddenly, Jasmine knew just what to do for the talent show.

Chapter Six

Jasmine's Big Surprise

The next morning, Jasmine rippled with renewed energy.

"Mom," she asked, "Will you drive me to the craft store?"

"Sure, honey," her mom said. "What do you need from the craft store?"

"Something for the talent show. It's a surprise." Jasmine pulled on a hoodie and ran to the garage. Her mom had still been in her pajamas when Jasmine asked her for a ride, so it took a while before Mom came out.

In the car, Jasmine kept looking out the window. She asked, "Can you drive faster?"

"You must be really excited about this," Mom said.

Jasmine's cheeks blushed in bright shades of pink and red. "I can't wait!" she said. For the next four days, Jasmine closed herself up in her room. No sounds could be heard from outside her door.

"What are you doing in there?" May and Sophie called, knocking.

From inside her room, Jasmine shouted, "It's a surprise!"

May giggled. "You're being so secretive!"

Finally, the day of the big talent show arrived. Jasmine's sisters loaded their guitars into the back of the family minivan, while Jasmine carried a suitcase out to the car.

"I hope you haven't picked 'take a fancy vacation without us' as your talent," Dad joked. Jasmine rolled her eyes. "You girls always roll your eyes at my jokes, but I'm pretty funny. In fact, I considered a stand up comedy act instead of the Amazing Armstrongs this year."

"Stick to music, Dad," May groaned.

"This year, maybe. But next year I'm

thinking about shaking it up. A cooking demonstration, or unicycle act…"

Jasmine's family buckled into their seats.

"Mom, did you invite Antonia and Carlos?" Jasmine asked.

"They'll be there," Mom said, and smoothed Jazzy's unruly curls.

"Good!" Jasmine said, bursting with excitement.

In the crowded auditorium, kids and parents filled the seats while the acts milled around backstage. With one hand, Jasmine picked up a program and scanned the numbers. There were The Amazing Armstrongs, a magic act, several dancers and solo singers, one piano piece, an acrobat, a comedienne and a group of kids performing a scene from Hamlet. Jasmine found her own name in the music section where she was listed next to the word "Tuba." But Jasmine wasn't going to play the tuba.

"It looks like a great line up!" Sophie said.

"It does, but…" Jasmine squinted as she re-read the program.

"What's wrong?" Sophie looked over

Jasmine's shoulder.

Shaking her head, Jasmine asked, "Where's Alec's name?"

Backstage, the crowd was jam-packed as Jasmine pushed through, searching for Alec. It was especially hard to wind her way around people while she carried her suitcase in one hand and the program in the other. She found Alec inside a small practice room. Alec's sandy curls had been combed into careful waves. He wore a colorful jacket and baggy, striped pants.

"You look great!" Jasmine gushed.

Alec dipped his head. "Thanks, Jazzy," he said. His words came out in a whisper.

"Hey," she said. "Why aren't you in the program?"

Three girls in a wide, green tutus stumbled past Alec and Jasmine. "Sorry!" they sang out.

"I'm sure it's just a mistake," Alec shrugged. Nearby, a man tuned his fiddle.

Just then, Greta and Haley walked past the doorway of the small room Alec and Jasmine stood in.

"Hi!" Jasmine poked her head out of the

doorway. "Greta! Haley!" The girls turned around.

"Hey Jazzy," Haley said. She walked back towards Jasmine, taking in her white t-shirt and black leggings. "Is that what you're wearing in the show?"

"Oh," Jasmine skimmed her outfit. "No, I'm not dressed yet. But you look really fancy!"

A tiara sat upon Haley's head and she wore a lavender suit with a sequined purple scarf.

"Thank you," Haley said.

Jasmine fumbled with her suitcase's handle. "Um, hey. Do you know why Alec isn't in the program?"

"Isn't he?" Haley raised her eyebrows just a tiny bit. Haley craned her head around the doorframe, locking eyes with Alec. "Did you really mean to breakdance in the show, Alec?"

"Absolutely," he said.

"Oh," Haley said. "I guess I thought you were joking. I'll make sure to announce you then."

"Thanks," Jasmine said.

"Yeah, thanks." Alec's face looked pinched.

53

Haley adjusted her tiara. "But he'll have to be last because he isn't in the program," she said to Jasmine. Haley and Greta walked away.

"Break a leg," Jasmine muttered under her breath. This was what you were supposed to say to wish performers good luck before they went onstage. Alec burst into laughter.

"What?" Jasmine asked. Then she began laughing too.

"Places everyone!" Greta called out.

Chapter Seven
Talented Turn of Events

The first act was *The Amazing Armstrongs*.
Playing two catchy folk songs, they sang along
in perfect harmony. Next, Mrs. McClure, a
cashier from Jasmine's grocery store, performed
a piano piece. The third act was the green tutu'd
ballerinas. Several more acts performed before
a short intermission. Jasmine's heart thudded
through her small body. Finally, Jasmine was up
next.

The stage stayed dark as Haley announced,
"Next up, Jazzy Armstrong!"

A shimmering lightsaber raced to life on the
black stage. Jazzy swooped it in a circle. The

theme to *Star Wars* slowly rose in volume as the lights came up. Center stage, Jazzy wore her classic, white Princess Leia costume from last year's Halloween. She whipped her lightsaber as if she were battling a Sith enemy. Bringing her lightsaber above her head, she then slashed it down.

"Ha ha!" she shouted. "You will never harm another Jedi again!" The violins picked up the pace of the music as Jazzy nodded to Greta offstage. Greta turned up the volume. Then she piped in a blue mist from the offstage fog machine, giving the scene an otherworldly radiance. Jazzy threw her head back and slipped the white robe from her shoulders, revealing her beautiful, hand-sewn Cloud City costume underneath.

"Ohhhh!" The audience gasped. A wave of delight raced through Jasmine's body. Her act was a hit! Jazzy spun in a slow circle, showing the intricate patterns on the dazzling cape.

"Whoo hoo!" her dad shouted from the audience. Other people clapped too. Jazzy gave one final spin as the music ended and the lights went black. She did it! Running offstage, she could still hear the audience clapping. Jazzy held her hand across her mouth to keep from laughing out loud.

She had been amazing! Jazzy took a deep breath and turned to watch the rest of the show.

At the edge of the stage, she watched Haley return to the microphone. Just behind Haley, Alec waited in the wings on the opposite side of the stage.

"Well, folks, that was a great show! We want to thank all of the performers and…"

Jazzy's ears filled with a sort of roaring sound. Haley wasn't going to announce Alec. Haley was ending the show!

Jazzy looked at the sound box hanging to her right. Before she could stop herself, she reached over and flipped the switch marked "mic" to the off position. Haley continued talking but no one could hear her. She frowned and then tapped the microphone.

Jasmine bit her lip, flipped the switch back on, and ran onstage. "Hi everyone!" she said, leaning into the microphone. "Haley forgot to announce the best act of all! Please give a big hand to our finale, Alec Waldon in his wheelchair breakdance routine!"

Jazzy dashed backstage to find Greta. "Cue Alec's music!" she said.

Greta frowned. "I don't have any music for Alec."

"But Alec gave Haley his music…" Jazzy had to find some music for Alec.

"Put my music on again!" Jazzy said.

"The Star Wars theme?" Greta asked.

Jazzy looked at Alec. "Will that work?" she

asked.

Alec smiled. "It's perfect!"

"Cue the music!" Jasmine said. Greta ran towards the sound booth.

Alec wheeled onstage.

The first few bars kicked in and Alec's strong shoulders began pumping up and down in time with the music. He spun, backed up and popped a wheelie! Then Alec turned his wheelchair completely on its side, holding his weight and the weight of his chair with one arm! From backstage, Greta began flashing colored lights across the stage as Alec danced.

He swiveled the chair back and forth, twisting, turning and lifting it off the ground in short hops. The audience went wild, clapping and whistling for Alec. As the music soared, he pressed both hands into the floor and lifted his body, and his whole wheelchair, over his head!

The audience jumped to their feet. Alec had completed a perfect handstand! People shouted and clapped, whistled and punched the air in awe of Alec's dance. Jazzy's heart felt like it was trying to burst from her chest. Alec flipped

his chair back down and took a bow. Then he looked at Jazzy. She gave him a thumbs up and Alec's face broke out in a grin that would rival any sunny day.

After the show, Jazzy looked for her family.

"Hey," a boy stepped in front of her. "You were great!" Jazzy didn't know him, but she liked the Return of the Jedi backpack that hung off his shoulder.

"Thanks," she said. A man and woman stood behind the boy. Their skin was pale, like Jazzy's parents and sisters, but the boy had dark skin.

"We loved your act!" the lady said. Jazzy looked from the couple to the boy. He glanced back.

"Oh," he said. "I'm Michael and these are my parents."

"Are you adopted?" Jazzy blurted.

Michael's smile faded a bit. Maybe, like Jazzy, he was tired of people asking him that.

"Because I'm adopted!" Jazzy added quickly, surprised at how easily it came out.

Michael's eyebrows rose up. "I don't know anyone else who's adopted!"

"Me neither!" Jazzy said.

"I'm new here. My mom and dad adopted me from foster care in North Carolina."

Jazzy was about to ask the boy for his phone number when Antonia threw her arms around her. "Where did you learn to sew like that?" she asked.

"You looked like a real Jedi fighter!" Carlos hung off Jasmine's arm.

"I can't believe how gorgeous that cape is," May said. "Can I borrow it?"

Jazzy looked behind her for the boy who was adopted and liked Star Wars. "Mom!" she said. "I met a boy who..." But the boy and his family were gone.

Jasmine's mom squeezed her shoulders. "I'm so proud of you," she said. "How did you get to be so amazing?"

"Well…" Jasmine had one more surprise for her family.

She dug a photo out of the pocket of her cape. It was the picture of her birth and adoptive family from the Walnut Room dinner. "I guess I got it from my amazing family," she said and leaned into their warm, strong hugs.

Glossary of Terms

Birth Mother – The biological mother of an adoptee.

Birth Brother – The biological brother of an adoptee.

Open Adoption – An adoption where the birth family and the adoptive family have some form of contact. This could be as simple as knowing each other's names or as involved as regular visits.

Abuela – The Spanish word for grandmother.

Wheelchair breakdancing – The art of breakdancing while seated in a wheelchair. One of the most famous wheelchair breakdancers is Maksim Sedakov, who is able to perform amazing feats in his wheelchair.

Foster care – Foster care is a temporary home for children who need a safe place to live when their parents or legal guardians are unable to take care of them. Their families often struggle with many difficult conditions.

Other adoption-related books published by Marcinson Press:

Awakening East: Moving our Adopted Children Back to China

Geezer Dad: How I Survived Infertility Clinics, Fatherhood Jitters, Adoption Wait Limbo, and Things That Go "Waaa" in the Night

The New Crunch-Time Guide to Parenting Language for Haitian Adoption

Ladybug Love: 100 Chinese Adoption Match Day Stories

Are You Ready to Adopt? An Adoption Insider's Look from the Other Side of the Desk

The New Crunch-Time Guide to Parenting Language for Chinese Adoption

Now available through Amazon.com, IndieBound.com, BarnesandNoble.com, and by request through major and independent bookstores.

For bulk purchases or
to carry this book in
your library, school, or
bookstore, please contact
the publisher at
www.marcinsonpress.com.

MARCINSON PRESS

CPSIA information can be obtained
at www.ICGtesting.com
Printed in the USA
LVOW04s0227211216
518200LV00007B/68/P

589

Karen's Book

Other books by
Ann M. Martin

P. S. Longer Letter Later
(written with Paula Danziger)
Leo the Magnificat
Rachel Parker, Kindergarten Show-off
Eleven Kids, One Summer
Ma and Pa Dracula
Yours Turly, Shirley
Ten Kids, No Pets
With You and Without You
Me and Katie (the Pest)
Stage Fright
Inside Out
Bummer Summer

For older readers:

Missing Since Monday
Just a Summer Romance
Slam Book

THE BABY-SITTERS CLUB series
THE BABY-SITTERS CLUB mysteries
THE KIDS IN MS. COLMAN'S CLASS series
BABY-SITTERS LITTLE SISTER series
(see inside book covers for a complete listing)

BABY-SITTERS
Little Sister

Karen's Book
Ann M. Martin

Illustrations by Susan Crocca Tang

A
LITTLE APPLE
PAPERBACK

SCHOLASTIC INC.
New York Toronto London Auckland Sydney

ISBN 0-590-50051-1

12 11 10 9 8 7 6 5 4 3 2 1   8 9/9 0 1 2 3/0

Printed in the U.S.A.   40
First Scholastic printing, August 1998

*The author gratefully acknowledges
Stephanie Calmenson
for her help
with this book.*

1

Is Anybody Home?

I was sitting at the kitchen table blowing bubbles in my milk. *Blubble. Blubble. Blubble.*

"Bubboos!" said my little sister, Emily Michelle.

I blew a little harder to impress her. The bubbles spilled over my glass, onto the table, and down to the floor.

"You made a mess," said David Michael, my stepbrother.

"I will help you clean up," said Nannie, my stepgrandmother. "Then I have to get back to work."

Nannie has her own candy-making business. She works out of our second kitchen. (It used to be our pantry.)

While Nannie and I were cleaning up, Emily decided to blow bubbles too. But she did not do it right. That is because she is only two and a half. Instead of blowing, she snorted up some of her milk. The next thing we knew, she was coughing up the milk and her cup was on the floor.

After cleaning up the new mess, Nannie took Emily back to the kitchen with her. That left David Michael and me. We had been playing together all morning. We were kind of tired of each other.

"I am going upstairs to read a book," said David Michael. That left just me.

Daddy was in his office working. He works at home, like Nannie. When the door to his office is closed it means I am not supposed to bother him if I can help it. (The door was closed.)

Elizabeth, my stepmother, was at her office downtown.

Mommy and Seth, who is my stepfather, and Andrew, who is my little brother (he is four going on five), were in Chicago. (I will tell you why very soon.)

Kristy, my stepsister, was at her friend Abby's beach house.

Charlie and Sam, my other stepbrothers, were at sleepaway camp. (They were counselors.)

My best friend Hannie Papadakis had gone to visit her aunt in the country. And my other best friend, Nancy Dawes, was with her family at the shore.

So I was alone on a Friday afternoon in August. I was B-O-R-E-D. That spells bored! I could not believe it. I am usually a very busy person.

Who am I? My name is Karen Brewer. I am seven years old. I have blonde hair, blue eyes, and a bunch of freckles. (I have more freckles in the summertime because of the sun.) I am a glasses-wearer. I have two pairs. I have a blue pair for reading. I have a pink pair to wear the rest of the time. I do not have prescription sunglasses yet. But maybe I will. That will make three pairs of glasses!

Anyway, that is who I am. The question now was, what am I going to do? Hmm . . . I know! I promised to tell you why Mommy, Seth, and Andrew are in Chicago. Are you ready? It is a long story.

2

A Tale of Two Cities

The story I have to tell you starts when I was very little. You already know some of it, but now I will tell you more.

Back when I was little, my family was little too. It was just Mommy, Daddy, Andrew, and me. We all lived together in a big house in Stoneybrook, Connecticut.

Then Mommy and Daddy started having troubles. They argued all the time. They tried to work things out but they just could not do it. So they explained to Andrew and me that they love each of us very much, but they could not live together anymore. And they got divorced. Mommy moved to a little house not far away in Stoneybrook. She took Andrew and me with her. Then she met Seth. She and Seth got married, which is how Seth became my stepfather. My family had grown a little bigger.

After the divorce, Daddy stayed in the big house. (It is the house he grew up in.) He met Elizabeth and they got married. Elizabeth had been married once before and had four children. They are my stepsister and stepbrothers, Kristy, David Michael, Sam, and Charlie. Kristy is thirteen and the best stepsister ever. David Michael is seven, like me. And Sam and Charlie are so old they are in high school.

After awhile Daddy and Elizabeth adopted Emily from a faraway country called Vietnam. That is when Nannie came to live with us.

Nannie is Elizabeth's mother. She came to help out with Emily, but she really helps the whole family.

So that is how I started out with a little family and wound up with a big family. And I have not even told you about the pets yet. There are lots of them!

Midgie is Seth's dog, and Rocky is Seth's cat. Emily Junior is my pet rat. (I named her after Emily, of course.) Bob is Andrew's hermit crab.

The pets at the big house are Shannon, David Michael's Bernese mountain dog puppy; Scout, our training-to-be-a-guide-dog puppy; Boo-Boo, Daddy's cranky old cat; Crystal Light the Second, my goldfish; and Goldfishie, Andrew's llama . . . I mean fish.

Andrew and I used to switch houses almost every month. We spent one month at the big house and one month at the little house.

I gave us special names because we each have two of so many things. I started calling us Andrew Two-Two and Karen Two-Two. (I thought up those names after my teacher,

Ms. Colman, read a book to our class. It was called *Jacob Two-Two Meets the Hooded Fang*.)

We each have two families with two mommies and two daddies. We have two sets of toys and clothes and books. And we both have two bicycles, one at each house. I also have two best friends, Hannie and Nancy. Hannie lives across the street and one house over from the big house. Nancy lives next door to the little house.

Then came Chicago, which is why I started to tell you this story in the first place. What happened is that Seth, who is a carpenter, was offered an excellent job in Chicago that would last for a few months. He tried commuting for a while. That means he flew back and forth between work in Chicago and home in Stoneybrook. That was hard on all of us. So Mommy, Seth, Andrew, me — plus Midgie, Rocky, Emily Junior, and Bob — moved to Chicago. Now I had two cities on top of everything else — Stoneybrook and Chicago.

But I missed being in Stoneybrook very much. So I moved back. And here I am alone in the kitchen at the big house and I am B-O-R-E-D, which spells bored. What am I going to do now?

3

Karen's Idea

I decided David Michael had a good idea when he went upstairs to read. I went to my room to do the same thing. And I knew just the book I wanted to read.

Kristy had been reading some of the Little House books to me. (I told you she is the best stepsister ever.) The Little House books were written by Laura Ingalls Wilder, and they tell about her life. She was a real and true American pioneer. I love her books.

I picked up the first one, *Little House in the Big Woods*, and looked at the pictures. When she was a little girl, Laura lived with her ma, pa, and two sisters in a small log cabin. Her pa built the cabin himself. It was a lot smaller than my little house, but five people lived in it.

The three girls slept in trundle beds. (Those are little beds that slide underneath a big bed.) They helped their ma make cheese and butter. Their pa hunted, farmed, played his fiddle, and sang to his family. Laura Ingalls Wilder had a happy and exciting life.

I thought of someone else I know who has a happy and exciting life — well, most of the time. Me!

I do not sleep in a trundle bed or churn butter (except once, for a school cooking project). But I do other exciting things.

Hmm. Maybe I could write the story of *my* life the way Laura Ingalls Wilder wrote the story of hers. Only I would illustrate my story too. The book would be about me, Karen Brewer, and my family and friends because they are part of my life too. Ooh! This was a gigundoly good idea.

Where would I start? I decided to start with the day I was born. That was a long time ago. Seven years. I did not remember much. In fact, I did not remember anything about the day I was born. Mommy and Daddy had told me stories, though. And I knew Daddy had pictures. I needed to do some research.

I ran downstairs to Daddy's office. His door was still closed.

I stood there deciding what to do. Knock. Do not knock. Knock. Do not knock.

Finally I felt as though I would burst if I did not knock on the door. Bursting would be an emergency situation. I knew Daddy would not want me to burst. Okay. I had to knock. I could not help it.

Knock, knock!

"Come in," replied Daddy.

I opened the door a crack and peeked in.

"I am sorry to bother you when you are working," I said. "But I really could not help it."

"That is all right," said Daddy. "I was just

about finished anyway. What can I do for you?"

"You can help me with some research," I replied.

"Sure," said Daddy. "What kind of research?"

"I am going to write my life story. I need to look at my baby book."

"You have come to the right place," said Daddy. "I keep it here in my office."

Yes! I was going to start my research right away. And I did not even have to burst.

4

Karen's History Lesson

My baby book was white with pink lettering. The very first page was titled BABY'S FAMILY TREE. I had not seen it in a long time.

"There are a few branches missing from this tree," I said.

"You are right," Daddy replied. "Your tree has grown since Mommy and I wrote in this book."

It was still fun to look at. I found names of people I know and love, and names of people I have never met. But they were all part of my history. I turned the page. There was a picture of me as a smiling baby.

"Hey, I was cute!" I said.

"You still are," replied Daddy.

"You know what is funny? I had no hair in the picture, but I have a lot now. You and Mommy had lots of hair in the picture, but you do not have so much now," I said.

"Karen Brewer, did you take my hair?" asked Daddy, joking. "I want it back!"

I leafed through a few more pages. I saw myself growing bigger and bigger.

"May I borrow the book?" I asked.

"Of course you may," replied Daddy. "I also have some other things that might interest you."

He pulled out a box and opened it. It was full of drawings I made when I was little. Some of them were just scribbles.

"You were a very good artist for your age, Karen," said Daddy. "You were a good writer too. You could not write down the words yourself, but you told your stories to

Mommy and me. We wrote them down for you."

Daddy showed me one of my stories. It was about shopping at the supermarket with Mommy.

Karen go to market with Mommy. Buy milk. Buy eggs. Buy cookies. Eat cookies! Love cookies! The end.

"Thank goodness I am a better writer now," I said. "Okay. I need to know all about the day I was born. I know you and Mommy have told me the story lots of times. But I may have forgotten some things."

"Ask me any questions," said Daddy. "I will answer the best I can."

"Okay," I replied. "Here goes."

I had a long list of questions. I wanted to know exactly what the weather was like on the day I was born. What time was I born? How much did I weigh? How tall was I? Who were my first visitors? Did I cry much?

I asked Daddy all my questions and he answered them for me one by one. We even called Mommy in Chicago to see if there was anything else she wanted to tell me. By the time we were done, I knew the whole story of the day I was born. And I had lots of other stories too.

Decisions, Decisions

I carried my baby book upstairs. I was ready to begin writing. Watch out, Laura Ingalls Wilder!

I grabbed a pencil and a sheet of paper from my desk. I looked at the pencil and paper. They were not in great shape. The pencil was short and chewed. (I wondered whose pencil it was. I do not chew my pencils.) Hardly any eraser was left. And the sheet of paper I picked was creased in one corner.

I decided I was not ready to begin writing

after all. A person's life story is a very important document and it should be beautifully written.

I found a brand-new pencil. It was pink with white flowers. Nannie had given it to me the week before. (Nannie was not even on my family tree. I would have to fix that.) Then I found clean paper with no creases.

I took my paper and pencil to my bed. It is a cozy place to write.

"Move over, please, Moosie and Goosie," I said.

Moosie and Goosie are my stuffed cats who look exactly the same. Goosie usually lives at the little house, but was with me at the big house while the rest of my family was in Chicago. I was glad Moosie and Goosie were getting along so well.

I puffed up my pillows and leaned back. I was finally ready. In the middle of the first page, I wrote in big letters:

MY LIFE STORY
BY KAREN BREWER

I took another sheet of paper and wrote at the top:

THE DAY I WAS BORN

Then I began my story.

IT WAS A DARK AND STORMY NIGHT WHEN...

No. That was not right. Daddy said I was born on a warm spring day. But that did not sound so exciting. Maybe the real and true story needed a little help. I tried again.

IT WAS THE MOST BEAUTIFUL SPRING DAY IN HISTORY. THE WEATHER ANNOUNCER WAS TALKING ABOUT HOW AMAZING THE WEATHER WAS ON THIS DAY.

Hmm. Maybe that was too much. Daddy had not said anything about the weather announcer. I tried again:

IT WAS A BEAUTIFUL SPRING DAY. PEOPLE EVERYWHERE WERE TALKING ABOUT IT. "WHAT A BEAUTIFUL DAY TO BE BORN!" SAID A MAN ON THE STREET. "YES, I WISH I COULD HAVE BEEN BORN ON A DAY LIKE TODAY," SAID A WOMAN.

I looked at Moosie and Goosie. I could tell

22

they did not believe my story. I erased the last three sentences. Here is what was left:

IT WAS A BEAUTIFUL SPRING DAY.

That was the real and true story. You know what? It was not a bad way to start. I decided to tell my story the way it really happened. All I had to do was figure out what to say next.

I looked at one of my baby pictures. I closed my eyes and made believe I was a baby again. I imagined everyone going wild. They were holding me, feeding me, and — *ooh!* — they were tickling me!

Wait a minute. I was going too fast. Before I was tickled, I had to be born. Mommy and Daddy had told me about that day lots of times. And now Daddy had answered my questions. I was finally ready to begin my story.

6

The Day I Was Born: Part One

It was a beautiful spring day. Mommy and Daddy were up bright and early even though it was the weekend.

"Good morning, Lisa," said Daddy. "How are you feeling?"

"I am fine, thank you," replied Mommy.

Daddy looked down at Mommy's belly.

"And how are you feeling this morning, Baby?" he asked.

Mommy smiled. "Baby seems to be just fine," she said.

"Would the two of you like me to make breakfast for you?" asked Daddy.

"We would love it!" replied Mommy.

Daddy made pancakes with sliced strawberries on top. He drank a cup of coffee. Mommy drank a glass of milk.

"Would you like to go for a walk?" asked Mommy. "It is beautiful out, and I am feeling restless."

"That sounds good to me," replied Daddy. "We can stop at some Saturday-morning yard sales. Who knows what we will find?"

Mommy put on a sweater. She could not button it because her belly was too big. Mommy and Daddy went outside, holding hands. It was still very early, but they were not the only ones out.

"Good morning!" called a gray-haired man, walking a gray-haired dog. "When do you think your baby will be born?"

"Any day now," replied Daddy proudly.

At the corner, a woman on her bicycle

stopped to wait for the light. She looked at Mommy and Daddy and smiled.

"What are you going to name your baby?" she asked.

"We are going to wait and meet our baby before we pick a name," said Mommy.

"Do you think it is a boy or a girl?" asked the woman.

"We will be happy either way!" said Daddy.

The light changed. "Good luck," called the woman as she rode ahead.

"Look, there is a sign for a yard sale up ahead," said Mommy.

The sale was in the backyard of a small house. Right away Mommy and Daddy saw something they both loved. It was a beautiful old rocking chair, sitting on the grass in the sun.

"We can rock our baby in that chair," said Mommy. "It is perfect!"

"I love that chair too," replied Daddy. "But I do not want to buy it now. Some people say it is unlucky to buy too many things for a baby before it is born."

"But the chair may not be here if we wait," said Mommy. "Anyway, it does not have to be for our baby. We have a big house and can always use an extra chair."

"Well, maybe you are right," said Daddy.

"No. We will wait," said Mommy. "We can always find another pretty chair."

Mommy and Daddy kept changing their minds. They were rocking back and forth like the you-know-what. Just then, the owner of the house saw them.

"Hi, folks," he said. "How are you today? I will be happy to answer your questions. I know this chair well."

"Oh, my," said Mommy. "I need to sit down. I hope you do not mind." She sat in the rocking chair.

Daddy knelt down beside her. "Are you all right?"

"I am fine. I think our baby is ready to be born. That is all," replied Mommy, smiling.

"Oh, my," said Daddy.

"Oh, my," said the man. "We will get you to the hospital right away."

Daddy helped Mommy into the man's car. Soon they were on their way. And so was I.

7

The Day I Was Born:
Part Two

I did not arrive for a few more hours. The doctor checked in on Mommy every fifteen minutes.

"You are doing fine," Dr. Bradley told Mommy. "It will not be long now."

Daddy and Mommy talked a lot while they waited — mostly about me, of course. Then, in the middle of a sentence, Mommy stopped and said, "Watson, it is time!"

Mommy and Daddy were very excited.

At 2:35 in the afternoon, I, Karen Brewer, was finally born. It was my first important job. And I love important jobs.

But I need to back up a little. My name was not Karen yet. Mommy and Daddy were still calling me Baby. They looked at their list of possible names. I could also have been Arlene, Joanna, Bethany, Katherine, or Erica. I like all those names. I would have had a very hard time deciding on one.

Mommy and Daddy looked at the list again. Then they looked at me.

"There is only one name that seems right to me," said Daddy. "That name is Karen. It means 'pure.' And seeing our baby, I feel pure joy."

"Me too," said Mommy. "It is the right name."

Then they kissed my cheeks and said, "Hello, Karen Brewer. Welcome to the world!"

Mommy stayed overnight at the hospital. Daddy went home and called lots of relatives and friends. They all came to the hospital the next morning for my day-after-

being-born party. Grandma and Grandpa Packett, Mommy's parents, were there.

"We cannot get enough of our new granddaughter!" they said.

Grandma Brewer was there too. (Daddy's father, my Grandpa Brewer, died before I was born.)

"You are the sweetest thing," said Grandma Brewer.

By the time everyone left, the room was filled with balloons and flowers and baskets of fruit. I was the star of the party. I love being the star! But I cannot remember one thing about it. I am sure I had a good time, though. Daddy took lots of pictures and I think I am smiling. (It is hard to tell because I am mostly covered up with a blanket.) Anyway, the pictures are in my baby book now.

In the afternoon Mommy and Daddy took me home. One of Daddy's friends had decorated the car with pink streamers. (There is a picture of the car in my baby book too.)

We were all buckled up. I sat in my own baby seat. Daddy drove extra carefully.

"I can hardly wait to get Karen settled in her new room," said Daddy as he turned the corner to our street.

"Look!" said Mommy. "Karen's new room is going to have something very special in it."

There it was. Sitting on the grass in the sun. The beautiful oak rocking chair.

Daddy helped Mommy and me out of the car.

"There is a note on the chair," said Mommy. She read it out loud:

This chair was in my family for a long time. My mother and father rocked me in it. I want the chair to have a special home. It belongs with you.
Your friend and neighbor,
John Washington

You know what? We still have that rocking chair. It is in the den and it is my very favorite chair.

8

Karen Says, "No!"

I forgot to tell one thing about the rocking chair. The way it looks now is not exactly the way it looked when we bought it. (Daddy says he will fix it up one of these days to look like new.) Here are some of the things that happened to it:

Shannon, David Michael's puppy, thought the bottom rung would be a good chewing stick, and she chewed it right off.

Once, when I was about two years old, I decided the chair would look pretty with pictures on the seat, so I found a pen and scribbled. (It was all I could do back then.) I pressed really hard and the scribbles are still there.

Then there was the time I rammed my toy car into the chair. If you look at the bottom, you can see where I hit it.

And once I sat in the chair with my doll and started rocking her.

"Ride, dolly, ride!" I said.

I rocked so hard I tipped the chair over. It banged into the window ledge. You can see those marks on the chair too.

"It sounds like I was a busy baby!" I said to Mommy and Daddy one day when I was still little.

"Yes, you were," replied Mommy. "You played with your toys, chased Boo-Boo, and put on lots of shows for Daddy and me."

"You were the center of attention most of the time," said Daddy.

I am sure I liked that a lot. I still like being the center of attention. I guess that is why I was not too happy when I found out a new baby was on the way. This is how I figured it out.

"Mommy is getting fat!" I said when I was two and a half.

Mommy said she was not getting fat. She said a baby was growing inside her. "Just the way you grew inside me."

"There is no new baby," I announced. "I am the baby."

"The new baby will be your brother or sister," replied Mommy.

"No. No brother. No sister. I am the baby."

"Your baby brother or sister will grow up to be your friend," said Mommy. "You can play together."

"No."

"You can tell each other secrets."

"No."

"We think of the new baby as a gift to you," said Daddy.

"Gift?" I said.

"That is right," said Mommy.

"You will get to be a big sister," added Daddy.

I liked that idea.

"So do you think you might like the new baby?" asked Mommy.

"No!" I replied.

Poor Mommy and Daddy. They tried very hard.

9

Karen Brewer, Big Sister

It did not matter whether I wanted a baby brother or sister. I was getting one anyway.

Here is what happened the day Andrew came home from the hospital. Mommy and Daddy told me some of those things. I remembered the rest all by myself.

Grandma and Grandpa Packett did not go to the hospital when Andrew was born. They were busy taking care of me. We had fun. I helped Grandma bake a welcome-home cake. I got to pour sugar and flour in a bowl. I got to mix them up with a big wooden spoon.

"Mmm. Mommy and Daddy will love the cake," I said.

After it was baked, Grandma wrote a message on top with blue icing.

"What does it say?" I asked.

I thought it would say, "Welcome Home, Mommy and Daddy." It did not. It said, "Welcome Home, Andrew!"

"No!" I cried. I reached out to wipe the letters off with my finger. Grandma picked up the cake before I could get to it.

"You must wait to eat the icing on the cake," she said. "But you may lick it out of the bowl."

By the time I finished, my face was covered with blue icing and I had forgotten about the message on the cake.

"Who wants a horsey ride?" asked Grandpa Packett.

"Me!" I said.

I climbed on Grandpa Packett's back.

"Giddyap!" I called. We galloped around

the house. I was still on his back when I heard the key in the door. Daddy hurried in and swooped me up in a big hug. Then I looked at Mommy. She was carrying my baby brother.

He was wrapped in a yellow blanket. It looked like *my* baby blanket. That was the first problem. The second problem was his face. It was a red, wrinkly prune face.

"This is Andrew, your new baby brother," said Mommy.

I squirmed out of Daddy's arms and ran away crying. That made the baby cry. Mommy carried him inside and sat down in the rocking chair.

"*My* chair!" I said. I cried harder.

Mommy handed Andrew to Daddy. Then she took me on her lap and rocked me till I stopped crying.

"It is all right. You do not have to be happy about having a brother now," said Mommy. "You are a good girl and Daddy and I love you very much. We always will."

We rocked together in the chair for a long time.

Things got better after that. People came over with presents for Andrew. Sometimes they brought presents for me too!

Then one day Andrew started crying and would not stop. Mommy had fed him. Daddy had changed him. It was not his nap time. Grandma Packett was there.

"Call the doctor," she said.

"I do not think he is sick," said Mommy.

"He was all right a minute ago," said Daddy.

While they were talking, I tiptoed to Andrew's crib. I looked down at him. He was crying so hard that his face was purple. He looked like a purple, wrinkly prune. He opened his eyes and stared at me. I made a wrinkly prune face at him.

Andrew stopped crying. I made an even funnier face. Andrew smiled. Mommy, Daddy, and Grandma Packett ran to us.

"What happened?" asked Mommy. "Andrew looks fine now."

"I think his big sister helped him," said Daddy.

"Thank you, Karen," said Mommy. She hugged me.

I looked at Andrew again. He did not look like a purple prune anymore. He looked pink and kind of cute. I, Karen Brewer, his big sister, had made him stop crying. I felt like a Gigundoly Important Person. I decided that being a big sister might not be so bad after all.

10

Little Friends
Day School

Being the big sister has always meant doing a lot of things first. I got born first. I got rocked in the rocking chair first. I got to use the crib first. And I got to go to school first.

On my first morning of school, I was sitting at the breakfast table with Mommy, Daddy, and Andrew, who was in his high chair.

"I am going to Little Friends Day School," I said to Andrew. "You are too young to go to school."

"Ga, ga," replied Andrew. He was too young to talk.

"I am glad you are looking forward to school, Karen," said Mommy. "I think you will have fun."

"You will color and look at books," said Daddy. "You will dance and sing and make new friends."

I could hardly wait! I ate my cereal as fast as I could. I liked Krispy Krunchies. I still do. Only when I was little I did not like them crunchy. So Mommy poured the milk onto the cereal before I sat down at the table. That way it was nice and soggy when I was ready to eat it.

"Come, Karen," said Mommy. "We do not want to be late on your first day of school."

I put on my new Ms. Frizzle backpack. There was not much in it. A snack and maybe a pencil. But I loved it. It made me feel grown-up.

Mommy was going to drive me to school. We climbed in the car and buckled up. I waved good-bye to Andrew. If he could have, I bet he would have said, "I want to go to school too!"

But I am the big sister. So I got to go.

I thought school would be great. I liked our bright, sunny room. I saw lots of games and books.

My teacher, Ms. Herman, was very nice. She talked to us. She gave me my own cubby with my name on it. I hung my Ms. Frizzle bag on the hook. Then Mommy hugged me.

"Have a good time. I will pick you up at eleven-thirty," she said.

That is when I stopped liking school. Mommy tried to leave. I grabbed her leg and would not let her go.

"Karen, what is wrong?" asked Mommy.

"I want you to stay with me," I replied.

"Mothers do not go to school," said Mommy. "I have to go home and take care of Andrew."

"Why does Andrew get to stay home? I want to stay home too," I said. "I am scared to stay here alone."

"You are not alone. Ms. Herman is here. And there are lots of other children. They can be your friends."

Just then a little girl ran across the room to me. She slipped her hand in mine.

"Hi, my name is Hannie. Do you want to play?" she asked.

I had seen Hannie before. She had just moved into my neighborhood. She seemed nice. And she was not scared.

I turned to Mommy.

"You will not forget to pick me up, will you?" I asked. (Hey, I was only a little kid. I would not be such a scaredy-cat today.)

"Of course I will pick you up," said Mommy. "I will be here at eleven-thirty."

"Come on," said Hannie. "I want to build a block castle."

"We can build towers and bridges," I said.

And that is what we did. We built towers and bridges. We sat together at story time and snack time. I had a new school and a new friend too.

11

Karen's Tea Party

Hannie and I became best friends. We played together all the time. We were so glad we lived across the street from each other.

That is why I was extra sad when Mommy and Daddy got divorced and I had to move away. On moving day, Hannie came to say good-bye.

"I will never see you again!" she cried.

"You will see each other every day at school," said Daddy.

"I will call you." I sniffled.

"I will drive you here to visit," said Mommy. "And I am sure Hannie's mommy and daddy will drive her to our new house. It is not so far away."

Mommy and Andrew and I climbed into our car. I thought we were going to drive to the other end of the earth. But you know what? The ride took only a few minutes.

I really did miss having my best friend close by, though. One day I wanted to have a tea party. If Hannie and I still lived across the street from each other, Mommy could have walked me to her house. But Mommy was busy and could not stop to drive me. And Hannie's father had taken their car to the repair shop.

"I guess we could have our tea party on the phone," I said.

"It will be a little hard to pass the cookies," said Hannie. "Anyway, I have to hang up now. Mommy is waiting for a call."

"Okay, see you at school," I said.

Boo. I wanted to have a tea party. I decided I would just have to have one by myself. I took my tea set and a tablecloth outside. I ran inside and got juice and cookies. I spread everything out on the front lawn. I was ready for my first guest.

"Dingdong!" I said.

"Coming!" I replied.

I opened my make-believe front door for my make-believe guest.

"Hello," I said. "I am so glad you could come for tea. Hannie is sorry she could not make it. Of course, that means we will have extra cookies."

I guess that was not very polite. But my guest did not seem to notice. At least she did not say anything.

I showed my make-believe guest to her seat.

"So, what is new?" I asked in my make-believe-guest voice. I ran to the other side of the tablecloth to answer myself.

"School was fun today," I said. "We read a book called *Alice's Tea Party*. It was excellent. Are you ready for some tea and cookies?"

I ran back to my make-believe-guest seat to answer.

"Thank you, I would love some," I replied to myself.

I ran back to the other side to pour the tea and pass the cookies. I was getting tired of running back and forth. I stopped for a minute to eat a cookie.

That is when I noticed a girl on the lawn next door. She was standing all by herself, giggling. I wondered what was so funny. Then I realized it was me. I must have looked pretty silly running back and forth. I started laughing too.

Then I thought of something. Having a real, live guest would be a lot more fun than talking to myself.

"Hi!" I called. "Would you like to come to my tea party? I have plenty of cookies."

"Thank you!" the girl called back. And she headed my way.

12

The Name Game

"I never saw anyone have a tea party like that before!" said the girl.

"I usually have tea parties with my friend Hannie. But Mommy could not drive me to her house," I replied.

"Where does she live?" asked the girl.

I told her about my old street. Then I told her about moving and how Mommy and Daddy got divorced. I told her about school and Andrew.

She told me about the school she went to and about her mommy and daddy. She said she did not have any brothers or sisters or pets.

"I want to get a cat someday," she said. Then she added, "Hey, I do not even know your name."

"And I do not know yours," I said. "This is fun! We can guess each other's names."

"Okay," said the girl. "You look like Susan."

"Wrong!" I said. "My turn. You look like Elizabeth."

"Nope," said the girl. "I bet your name is Carol."

When I heard "Ca" I thought she was going to guess my name.

"Close, but wrong again!" I said. "Give me a hint, and then I will give you one."

The girl stopped to think. Then she said, "The second part of my name is something you do with your eyes."

"Blink!" I shouted. "Your name is Roblink!"

"No way!" said the girl, giggling. "Now you have to give me a hint."

"My name starts like the name you guessed last time," I said.

"Um, Susan? Is your name Suellen?" said the girl.

"No. Susan was your first guess. Okay, now it is my turn," I said. "You *see* with your eyes. Your name is Tracy!"

"No, it is not," said the girl. "I remembered the name I guessed. It was Carol. Your name is Katherine!"

Just then, my mother opened the door and stepped out. Before I could stop her, she called, "Karen, are you ready for some lunch?"

"I got your name! It is Karen and I am a genius!" said the girl.

"Very funny," I replied. "Now you have to tell me your name."

"I do not. I want you to guess it."

"You did not guess my name. If you want to be my friend, you have to tell me yours," I said.

The girl was quiet for a minute. Then she said, "My name is Nancy."

"That is a nice name," I said.

"I like yours, too."

Then I called, "Mommy, can Nancy come for lunch?"

"Of course," replied Mommy.

Nancy ran home to make sure that was okay. It was. She ate lunch at my house. I ate dinner at hers.

I felt like the luckiest kid in the world. Now I had two great friends, and one of them lived right next door.

13

Goosie and Moosie

After awhile I got used to living at the little house and visiting the big house. But it was not so easy at the beginning. I did not like leaving Mommy. And sometimes I would forget things at one house or the other. (I was not a true two-two yet.) The first time Andrew and I went back to the big house, I forgot my toothbrush.

"We have plenty of extras," said Daddy.

I chose a pink-and-blue-striped one. It was pretty, but it was grown-up size and too big for my mouth.

Another time I forgot my pajamas. Hannie was sleeping over anyway, so she brought me a pair of hers.

But there were two things I *always* needed to have with me. I needed Tickly, my special blanket, and Goosie, my stuffed cat. I could not sleep without them.

One night Daddy was tucking me in at the big house.

"Wait, I have to find Tickly," I said.

I looked on my bed. No Tickly. I looked on the floor. No Tickly. I looked all around my room. No Tickly!

"We will find it in the morning," said Daddy.

"I have to have Tickly now," I said.

We looked everywhere but could not find Tickly.

"We have to go back to the little house," I said.

"All right, Karen. Put your coat on over your pajamas and we will go," said Daddy.

By the time we were downstairs, I was crying and cranky. So was Andrew. Daddy was unhappy because it was way past my bedtime. But we were going to go back to the little house anyway. We just had to. I opened the car door. The light came on.

"Tickly!" I shouted. My blanket was on the floor of the car. "I knew I did not forget you!"

"Well, that is a good thing," said Daddy.

We hurried back upstairs. I undressed and went to sleep with Tickly on my right side and Goosie on my left.

The next morning, I tore Tickly in half. I took half to the little house and left half at the big house. That way I would never be in either place without my special blanket. Unfortunately, the next week I forgot Goosie.

"Oh, Karen, not again," said Daddy.

"At least it is not bedtime," I replied. (I realized Goosie was missing as soon as we got to Daddy's house.)

"Maybe Goosie is in the car. Remember when you thought you lost Tickly?" said Daddy. We looked in the car. But Goosie was not there.

"I will drive you over to Mommy's," said Daddy.

At Mommy's house, Daddy rang the bell. Mommy was not home. Daddy found his keys so we went inside. Goosie was not at the little house either!

"I lost Goosie!" I cried. "I will never see him again!" I began to cry.

"We will go back and look at the other house," said Daddy. "I am sure he is there."

I was still crying when we pulled into the big-house driveway. Mommy was just getting out of her car. She was holding Goosie.

"You left him in the living room when you ran back for your sweater," said Mommy.

"Thank you!" I said. I was very happy to have Goosie back. But I started crying all over again.

"What is wrong?" asked Mommy.

"I am afraid I will leave him behind again. And I cannot tear him in half like Tickly."

Mommy and Daddy had a grown-ups'

talk. When they finished, Daddy said, "Come, we will go downtown and see if we can find another stuffed cat like Goosie."

We drove to the toy store. There, behind all the other stuffed toys, was a cat that was Goosie's twin. Mommy and Daddy bought him for me.

"Thank you!" I said. On the way back to the big house, I named my new cat.

"Goosie, meet Moosie," I said when I was in my room.

My life as a two-two had begun.

14

Meeting Seth

"We have so many books in this house," said Mommy. "I think we need to have some bookcases built into our walls."

"I want to help," I said. "I build good castles."

"You are a very good builder, but I think we are too busy to do this ourselves," said Mommy. "I am going to call a carpenter."

Mommy looked in the phone book under C for *carpenters* and found an ad she liked.

"What does it say?" I asked.

Mommy read me the ad. (I was only four

and a half, so I could not read it myself yet.) It said:

Need something built or repaired?
For Fast, Friendly, Fair Service
Call Seth Engle
Licensed Carpenter

Mommy set up an appointment for ten o'clock Saturday morning. When the doorbell rang and Mommy opened the door, I was surprised. I do not know why, but I was expecting someone old. But the man at the door was only old like Mommy. They smiled at each other.

Then they talked about where the bookcases should go. Once they had decided, the carpenter said he could start as soon as he had the proper materials. He came back the next Saturday.

"Do you need me to help you?" I asked.

"I am sure you are a very good helper," he said. "But you have to ask your mommy. These tools can be dangerous."

"It is all right," said Mommy. "I will watch you."

The carpenter told us to call him Seth.

"You can call me Karen. My mommy's name is Lisa!" I said.

It was my job to pass Seth his tools. I had to be careful. The hammer was heavy and the nails were sharp. (It was good that Andrew was napping. He was too little to help with important building jobs.)

While Seth and I were working, Mommy and Seth were talking. They were laughing a lot too.

Seth worked until lunchtime. Then he said, "I have another job now. I will have to come back and finish this on Monday."

When he came back on Monday, we were just starting to fix dinner.

"Are you sure you can do the job without me?" I asked.

"It will be hard, but I will do my best," said Seth.

I liked Seth. I could tell Mommy did too. After he left, she looked sad. We were about to eat our dessert when the doorbell rang. It was Seth again.

"I am sorry to bother you. I forgot my hammer," he said.

"It is no bother," said Mommy. "Would you like to join us for dessert?"

"Thank you, I would love to," he replied.

We were having apple cake that Mommy, Andrew, and I had baked together.

"This is delicious!" said Seth.

On his way out, Mommy asked Seth if he could build bookcases in my room too. I did not even know I needed them.

"Sure. I see your stair railing needs mending too. I will do that for nothing," said Seth.

Seth came around a lot after that. Mommy kept thinking of things that needed building. And Seth found lots of things that needed fixing.

Hmm. Something was going on.

15

Flower Girl: Part One

One Sunday Seth came over without his toolbox. Instead he brought presents for Mommy, Andrew, and me. Andrew and I got silly animals made out of wood. We loved them. Mommy got three wooden flowers painted in bright colors.

"Thank you. These flowers are beautiful," she said.

Seth spent the day with us. We walked around downtown and stopped for ice cream. Later we bought food at the super-market and cooked dinner together.

Seth spent a lot of time with us after that. We really liked him and I knew he liked us. He even said he wanted to marry us! At first I was a little scared.

"What about Daddy?" I asked Mommy one night after Seth went home.

"You will always have your daddy, who loves you. Nothing will change that," replied Mommy.

She explained that if she and Seth married, Seth would be my stepfather. "Seth is another person who loves you and wants to take care of you," said Mommy.

That did not sound too bad to me. The next time Seth came over, I said, "Yes, we will marry you!"

Mommy and Seth laughed and hugged. Then came the fun part — the wedding! I got to be the flower girl. This was a very important job.

On the Sunday before the wedding we all had to go to the church and practice walking down the aisle. It was like getting ready for a school play. Only I did not get to say anything. At least I was not supposed to. But being quiet is hard for me.

"Should I walk fast or slow?" I called from the back of the church. Mommy came back and walked down the aisle with me.

"You need to walk slowly with the music," she said.

"Okay, now I will do it myself!" I said.

I ran to the back again. When the music started, I did not walk. I decided to skip. It is hard to skip slowly. I reached the front of the church in no time.

"Karen, we do not skip in church," said Mommy. "Please try walking again."

"But a wedding is happy," I said. "So is skipping."

"We need you to walk slowly so everyone can see how beautiful you look with the flowers," said Seth.

Seth always knows what is important. That is one of the reasons I like him. I ran to the back and called, "I am ready!"

The music started. I took one step and waited. Then I took another step and waited some more. I was only halfway down the aisle when the music ended.

"That was great," said Seth. "We can always play more music."

I practiced at home. I practiced at the Little Friends Day School. Finally, it was the day of the wedding.

"Do not be nervous," said Mommy.

"I am not nervous one bit!" I replied.

The church was filled with people. I could hardly wait for the music to begin. When it did, Mommy nodded and I started to walk down the aisle. I was wearing a gigundoly beautiful dress. It was long and pink with ruffles. I was carrying a big bouquet of flowers.

I did not walk too fast. I did not skip. I did not walk too slowly. I walked with the music, just like Mommy said. Everyone was smiling at me and I was smiling back.

It was the most fun day. After Mommy and Seth were married, it was time for the party. We held it outside in the park. (We

had tents in case it rained. But it did not. The weather was beautiful.)

We ate and danced and I got too many kisses. But I did not mind. After all, you have to expect lots of kisses when you are the best flower girl in Stoneybrook.

16

Kristy Thomas

One weekend, when Seth was away and Andrew and I were at Daddy's, Daddy got a phone call. He said hello, then got a worried look on his face.

I got scared. Daddy does not look worried very often.

"Daddy?" I said. I wanted to know what was wrong. Daddy motioned for me to wait. I started bouncing up and down. I could not stand still.

Then I heard Daddy say, "I will get someone to stay with Karen and Andrew. I will be over as soon as I can."

Daddy hung up and turned to Andrew and me.

"Everything will be all right," he said. "There is no need to worry, but Mommy hurt her ankle and she is at the hospital. I need to go there and help her."

Andrew started to cry.

Daddy took Andrew and me in his arms. "Mommy will be all right," he said. "Sometimes we fall. We may get hurt, but then we get better."

Daddy picked up the phone again and made a call.

"Hello, Elizabeth," he said. "Could Kristy baby-sit for Karen and Andrew? I can pick her up and bring her here."

(I had not met Elizabeth or Kristy yet.)

"Thank you," said Daddy. He hung up the phone. "Come on, kids. Someone very nice is going to stay with you."

We drove to a house on the other side of town and a girl got into our car.

"Hi, Karen. Hi, Andrew. I am Kristy. Your daddy has told me a lot of nice things about you."

"Hi!" I replied. I did not get to say much else. Daddy was doing all the talking. He was telling Kristy what we should have for lunch and where emergency phone numbers were.

"I wish I could take time to show you everything," he said. "Karen will have to fill in for me. Okay, pumpkin?"

"Okay!" I replied.

Daddy dropped us back at our house, then drove off to the hospital. Kristy, Andrew, and I went inside.

"Do not worry. I am a very good helper! I will show you everything in my house," I said.

"Maybe we should eat some lunch first," said Kristy.

That sounded like a good idea. I had eaten only a little breakfast. Toast and orange juice. I was hungry. Andrew said he was hungry too.

I went to the kitchen and started taking food out of the refrigerator. Cold cuts. Cheese. Tuna salad. Cole slaw. Apples. Carrots. Milk.

"Whoa! Your daddy said peanut butter and jelly sandwiches," said Kristy.

"That is for Andrew. I like everything!" I replied.

Kristy made sandwiches and cut up apples and carrots. She put the food on our plates so it looked very pretty.

"Yum!" I said. "You are a good baby-sitter."

"I have not done too much yet, but thank you," said Kristy. She poured the milk and we sat down to eat.

I took a few bites of my sandwich, then suddenly felt like crying. I looked at Kristy.

"Will our mommy be all right?" I asked.

"Of *course*," replied Kristy. "She hurt her ankle, but that is not too terrible a thing to happen. Even if she broke it, she will be okay. I once broke my ankle too."

"How did you do that?" I asked.

"While you are eating I will tell you," said Kristy.

I picked up my sandwich and took another bite. I was starting to feel better already.

"Here is my story," said Kristy. "I was riding my bike and my dog, Louie, was on his leash —"

"You have a dog?" I said. "Can I see him sometime?"

"Sure," said Kristy. "Anyway, I was taking Louie for a walk when —"

"Ooh! Can I walk him?" I asked.

"I guess," replied Kristy. "Are you going to let me finish the story?"

I nodded.

"All right, then. I was on my bike and Louie was beside me when I came to a tree. Louie went one way and I went the other. *Whoosh!* I flew off my bike and broke my ankle," said Kristy.

I started giggling.

"That was silly!" I said.

"It was not silly when I had to wear a cast

for six weeks and could not go swimming all summer," said Kristy. "But you are right. It sounds pretty silly now."

I liked Kristy. She was nice. I thought she was nice even before she gave Andrew and me ice cream for dessert.

After lunch, we played outside. Then, while Andrew was napping, Kristy read stories to me. We were reading *The Little Engine That Could* when Daddy walked through the door.

"Mommy is going to be fine. She is home and will call you soon," said Daddy. "How did everyone here get along?"

"Fine," I said. "I like Kristy! Does she have to go home?"

"Not yet. We have to wait for Andrew to wake up before I drive Kristy home," said Daddy. "Kristy, is that all right with you?"

"I do not mind at all," said Kristy. "Karen and I are having a very good time."

Kristy looked at me and smiled. I felt a lot better than before. Mommy was going to be fine. And I had the best baby-sitter ever.

The Witch's Spell

Kristy baby-sat for us lots of times after the day Mommy hurt her ankle. She got to know our house pretty well.

At first I only told Kristy nice things about our house. I wanted to be sure she came back. But on her third visit I decided to tell her about the witch next door. It was for her own safety.

"Um, I hope this will not scare you away," I said. "But there is a witch living next door."

"Really?" asked Kristy. She looked as though she did not believe me.

"Yes. Daddy thinks her name is Mrs. Porter. But her real name is Morbidda Destiny," I said.

"That *does* sound like a witch's name," said Kristy.

"She dresses in black and casts spells. Once she cast a spell on Boo-Boo. That is why he is wild," I went on.

"Well, then, I will watch out for Boo-Boo and for your neighbor. Thank you for warning me," said Kristy.

A couple of weeks later, Morbidda Destiny struck! Kristy was baby-sitting for Andrew and me. We were having a snack in the kitchen. Andrew was putting globs of jelly on crackers. And Kristy was looking for a jar of peanut butter when she bumped her head on a cabinet door.

"Ouch!" she said.

"Kristy get boo-boo!" cried Andrew.

Boo-Boo came into the room then. He must have thought Andrew was calling him. He rubbed against Andrew's chair.

Grape jelly from Andrew's crackers dripped onto Boo-Boo's tail. *Mee-owww!*

Boo-Boo licked his tail furiously. Then he started chasing his tail and would not stop. He jumped up on the counter, then down to the floor. Things were falling over. Boo-Boo was making a gigundo mess.

"Catch him!" I said.

"I will try my best," said Kristy.

She grabbed two oven mitts and put them on.

"No! I said catch him, not cook him!"

Kristy started to laugh. "I am putting the mitts on so I do not get scratched."

"Oh," I replied. Kristy was pretty smart.

But she was not smart enough to catch Boo-Boo. He ran out of the kitchen and into the living room. *Crash!*

Kristy, Andrew, and I peered around a corner to see what had broken. Oops. It was a blue vase.

"Boo-Boo running!" said Andrew.

"He is under a witch's spell!" I exclaimed.

"I think it is an angry cat spell," said Kristy. "Cats do not like having sticky jelly on their tails."

Boo-Boo was flicking his tail and spraying grape jelly all around the house.

"We will have to wait till he calms down," said Kristy.

Crash! Bam! Bang! Just then the telephone rang. Kristy answered it.

"Yes, Mrs. Porter. Everything is all right. Thank you," she said and hung up.

"Aha!" I cried. "It was Morbidda Destiny, checking on her spell!"

"I do not think so. Mrs. Porter called to see if we could use help. She heard all the noise," said Kristy.

"That is what she *said*. But I know better," I replied.

After Kristy hung up the phone, Boo-Boo stopped running around. I knew it was because Morbidda Destiny had called off her spell.

Boo-Boo sat down and licked the little bit of jelly that was left on his tail. Kristy cleaned up the house. I helped her. When we finished, Kristy said, "Except for the broken vase, everything looks fine."

"Until the next spell," I said. "I hope you were not too scared. Will you come back?"

"Of course I will come back," said Kristy. "I am not scared of crabby cats or witch's spells. And when things go wrong, I know I have a very good helper. Thank you, Karen."

Kristy looked at me and smiled. Even a witch's spell could not change that.

18

Flower Girl: Part Two

Not long after the witch's spell, Andrew and I met Elizabeth, David Michael, Sam, and Charlie.

We spent a lot of time together on weekends when Andrew and I stayed at Daddy's. So by the time Daddy told us he and Elizabeth were going to get married, we already felt like family.

By then, Andrew and I were also already two-twos. That is why I was not surprised that I was going to be a flower girl for a second time. (I am lucky. Some girls never get to be a flower girl even once.)

On the day of the wedding, I jumped out of bed.

"I am going to be a flower girl! Today is the day! Hooray!" I sang to Moosie.

I ate breakfast with Daddy and Andrew. Daddy gave us each a big hug.

"I will be pretty busy later," he said. "But you know where to find me if you need me. I love you both."

As we were finishing breakfast, Elizabeth, Kristy, and Nannie came over. (I had met Nannie a few times by then.) The four of us went to the spare bedroom. That way Daddy would not see Elizabeth getting ready. (Some people think it is bad luck for the groom to see the bride dressed before the wedding.)

Nannie helped me put on my dress. She had made it herself. It was short and yellow with lace on it. I had yellow shoes, white tights, and yellow and white flowers in my hair. I checked myself out in the mirror. I looked gigundoly pretty.

The wedding was going to be held in our backyard. The yard is big, so there was room for lots of people. As it turned out, there was one person too many. You will soon find out why.

When I was dressed, I went out to the yard. The guests were wearing their best clothes. There were flowers everywhere. (Daddy is a gardener and loves beautiful flowers.)

Kristy called, "Karen, come on! We are starting."

Suddenly I got butterflies in my stomach. Even though I had been a flower girl before, I was nervous.

Daddy stood in front of the minister. David Michael stood beside Daddy. (David Michael was the ring bearer.)

The rest of us were at the back of the yard. When the piano player began the wedding march, Sam said, "Here we go!" Sam walked Nannie down the aisle to her seat. Then he stood beside David Michael.

Kristy, the bridesmaid, was next. She walked down the aisle, then stood across from Daddy, David Michael, and Sam.

It was my turn. I started down the aisle. I tossed white rose petals first to one side, then to the other. I tried my best to walk in time to the music. Right foot, left foot. Toss, toss. Right foot, left foot. Toss, skip! Skip! Oops! I heard someone say I was adorable. I smiled and threw extra petals her way. I was having fun!

Elizabeth walked down the aisle behind me, holding Charlie's arm. Charlie brought her to stand beside Daddy.

The service began. I daydreamed through most of it. I woke up when I heard the minister say, "You may kiss the bride."

Daddy leaned over and kissed Elizabeth. Then people started getting up to congratulate them. That is when I screamed. Someone was heading in Daddy's direction holding a small box in her hand. It was Morbidda Destiny!

I started to shout, "Do not take it! It is a wedding spell!" Daddy covered my mouth with one hand. With his other hand, he reached out to take the box from his guest.

I was too scared to see what happened next. I pulled away from Daddy and ran to the house as fast as I could.

When I was brave enough to peek outside, Morbidda Destiny was gone and the wedding was going as planned. I found out later that a key ring was in the box. And no one seemed to be under any spells.

Morbidda Destiny is a witch for sure, but I think she is not a very good one. Except for Boo-Boo, none of her spells has worked yet. Thank goodness!

19

Ms. Colman's Class

Did you know that I am in second grade? Well, I am. Some kids my age are in first grade. I was in first grade for one week, then my teachers decided I belonged in second grade.

That is how I ended up in Ms. Colman's class. I love Ms. Colman. She is smart and nice. She never raises her voice, even though I give her lots of reasons to raise it. For example, sometimes I talk too loudly in class. Then Ms. Colman says, "Indoor voice, please, Karen." I try to remember that, but whenever I am excited I forget.

Ms. Colman is only one of the great things about my second-grade class. The other great thing is that Hannie and Nancy are in the class too. When I joined the class I got to sit next to them in the back of the room. Later, when I got my glasses, Ms. Colman moved me to the front so I could see better. But we are still together most of the time in school and out. That is why we call ourselves the Three Musketeers.

I remember the first day in Ms. Colman's class very well. It was an important day for me and for Hootie. Only Hootie did not know it yet. He was still in the pet store. And he was not even named Hootie. I will explain.

After I settled in that first day, Ms. Colman said, "Class, I have not forgotten about our problem."

I raised my hand. (Since it was my first day, I tried to behave myself.) "What problem?" I asked when Ms. Colman called on me.

Ms. Colman told me that the class had been trying to decide on a class pet.

"We cannot seem to choose between a hamster and a rabbit," said Ms. Colman. She said the class was going to vote again in case some kids had changed their minds.

I raised my hand again. A mean boy gave me a dirty look. But I did not care. I had already told him to leave me alone. And I told him, "You do not scare me." (The boy was Bobby Gianelli, by the way. He is not so much of a bully anymore.)

Anyway, I raised my hand and said, "What about a guinea pig? Guinea pigs are great pets. I played with one once. He was very, very friendly."

Guess what? The kids loved my idea!

"A guinea pig *would* be a good pet," said a girl. (It was Sara Ford, only I did not know her name yet.)

"I like guinea pigs," said a boy. (It was Hank Reubens.)

"Me too," said another girl. (It was Audrey Green.)

Ms. Colman wrote *guinea pig* on the chalkboard next to *rabbit* and *hamster*. Then she took a vote.

"How many of you want to get a guinea pig?" she asked.

There were sixteen kids in the class that day. Sixteen hands shot into the air. Yes!

A couple of days later we went to the pet store and picked out our guinea pig. We named him Hootie because he makes a loud whistling sound.

Hootie is happy in second grade. And so am I.

20

Karen's Book

I stopped writing my book and put down my pencil. My hand was stiff from writing so much. I shook it around.

It was late Sunday afternoon and the house was coming back to life. I had been writing for most of the weekend. I stopped for important things such as eating and sleeping. But the rest of the time I had stayed in my room and kept on writing. I did not mind because I was having so much fun.

"Hi, Karen," said Kristy, poking her head

around my door. "What did you do all weekend?"

I looked at all the pages on my bed.

"I wrote a book," I said.

"Really? That is amazing! Can I see it?" asked Kristy.

"Soon," I replied. "I am almost finished."

Kristy smiled and closed the door. I took out a special folder and put my book into it. I fastened the clasp and was about to write the title of my book on the front when there was a knock at the door.

"Hi, sweetheart," said Daddy. "Are you ready for dinner?"

"I will be down in a minute," I replied.

When Daddy left, I wrote the title of my book in big letters on the cover of my folder. Then I drew a picture and taped it below the title.

I went downstairs and slipped the book under my chair. I did not want anyone to see it until I was ready.

While we were passing around the

spaghetti, I said, "I have an announcement. After dinner I will be reading my book in the den. Whoever wants to hear it is invited."

"Are you going to read from a Paddington book?" asked Elizabeth.

"No, I am going to read my own book," I replied. "I wrote it all by myself."

"Then I want a front-row seat," said Daddy.

After dinner, everyone followed me into the den.

"Thank you for coming," I said. "I hope you like my story." (I heard an author say that at a bookstore once. I thought it sounded very nice.)

I held up my book and showed everyone the cover. It was a picture of me and my book. Then I began to read.

"*Little House, Big House: My Life Story*, by Karen Brewer," I said. Emily started clapping.

"Quiet, please. I have not even started the story yet," I said.

Nannie held Emily's hands in hers and I began to read.

" 'The Day I Was Born: Part One. It was a beautiful spring day,' " I said, and kept on going.

No one talked. No one fell asleep. Everyone listened. When I got to my last page, I read, " 'Hootie is happy in second grade. And so am I.' " Then I added, "The end. For now."

Daddy started clapping. Then Emily, of course. And Elizabeth, Nannie, Kristy, and David Michael.

"Bravo!" said Daddy. "I am so proud of you."

"That was a wonderful story," said Elizabeth.

"May I get a copy of your book?" asked Nannie. "I would like it signed by the author, please."

"So would I," said Daddy. "I will make copies for you. You can send one to Mommy, Seth, and Andrew in Chicago."

I could not believe it. I had written the

book just for fun. Now I felt like a real author.

"Everyone come to the kitchen for refreshments," said Elizabeth.

"I will come later. I want to write all this down," I said. I headed toward the stairs.

"Are you sure?" said Nannie. "We have cookies, ice cream, and homemade chocolates."

I turned back toward the kitchen.

"Yum! I want everything!" I said.

It was time for me to enjoy my first book party. Later, I could write all about it.

L. GODWIN

About the Author

ANN M. MARTIN lives in New York City and loves animals, especially cats. She has two cats of her own, Gussie and Woody.

Other books by Ann M. Martin that you might enjoy are *Stage Fright; Me and Katie (the Pest)*; and the books in *The Baby-sitters Club* series.

Ann likes ice cream and *I Love Lucy*. And she has her own little sister, whose name is Jane.

Little Sister

Don't miss #101

KAREN'S CHAIN LETTER

Hannie pointed. Oh my gosh! It was Ms. Agna! She was standing in our doorway talking to Ms. Colman. In her arms she held a big plastic sack.

"Karen?" said Ms. Colman. She motioned me to come over. She held the sack open for me to see. "Apparently you have received some mail at school," she said.

"My postcards!" I cried. "From my chain letter."

"Chain letter?" repeated Ms. Colman.

"Yes," I said. "It is sponsored by Kidsnetwork. These are postcards from all over the world!"

"Well," said Ms. Colman, "I can see that you are very excited. Perhaps you could share some of the postcards with the rest of the class."

LITTLE 🍎 APPLE

BABY-SITTERS™
Little Sister

by Ann M. Martin,
author of The Baby-sitters Club ®

More Titles... ➡